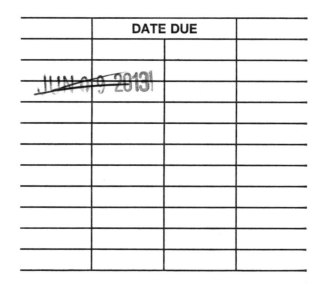

	DATE DUE		
	JUN 19 2013		

The Urbana Free Library

To renew: call 217-367-4057
or go to "*urbanafreelibrary.org*"
and select "Renew/Request Items"

The Berenstain Bears'
MOVING DAY

Their stuff is all packed!
Here comes the truck!
Let's move with the Bears
And wish them good luck.

A FIRST TIME BOOK®

The Berenstain Bears'
MOVING DAY

Stan & Jan Berenstain

Random House 🏠 New York

randomhouse.com/kids   BerenstainBears.com
Library of Congress Cataloging-in-Publication Data
Berenstain, Stan. The Berenstain bears' moving day.
(Berenstain bears first time books)
Summary: The Bear family decides it is time to move to a larger house.
ISBN 978-0-394-84838-9 (trade) — ISBN 978-0-375-98258-3 (ebook)
[1. Moving, Household—Fiction. 2. Bears—Fiction.] I. Berenstain, Jan. II. Title.
PZ7.B4483Bes [E] AACR2 81-50044
Printed in the United States of America   87 86 85 84 83 82 81 80 79 78 77 76

The Bear family didn't always live in the big tree house down a sunny dirt road deep in Bear Country.

Years ago, when Brother Bear was an only cub, they lived in a hillside cave halfway up Great Bear Mountain at the far edge of Bear Country.

It was a comfortable cave, cool in summer and cozy in winter. And while it wasn't perfect—it tended to be dark and it dripped and trickled a bit—it was *home,* and the Bear family was quite happy there.

Happy *and* busy.

Mama Bear kept busy managing things and tending the vegetable patch.

Papa Bear had plenty to do with his wood cutting and furniture making.

And Brother Bear kept busy climbing, collecting rocks, and playing with his friends.

But living on the mountainside wasn't perfect — it wasn't easy growing vegetables in the thin, rocky soil, and the trees Papa needed were getting fewer and farther between. But the sun was bright, the air was clear and sparkling, and the view was *magnificent!*

Yes, the Bear family was happy and content
living in their hillside cave halfway up
Great Bear Mountain at the far edge of Bear
Country. . . . Until one day, Papa Bear said,
"My dears, the time has come to move."

"Move!?" cried Brother Bear.

"That's right," said Papa. "The trees are getting few and far between on the mountainside."

"Yes," said Mama, "and it's not easy raising enough vegetables for a growing family in this thin, rocky soil."

"Where are we going to move *to?*" Brother asked.

"To the valley," said Papa as he began putting lamps and things into a box.

"The valley?" said Brother. The valley down there was nice to look at, but he wasn't so sure he wanted to live there. It was so far away.

"What about my toys?"
asked Brother.
"We'll take them along,
of course. Put them in here,"
said Papa, handing him a box.

"And what about my books?"
"We'll take them along, too," said Papa,
handing him another box.

"And what about my friends?" asked Brother. "We can't put *them* in a box and take them along!"

"That's true," said Mama, lifting Brother onto her lap. "You'll be leaving your friends behind. Papa and I will, too. That's what happens when you move. But you can keep in touch with them. You can write, even visit, perhaps. And besides, you can make lots of new friends."

"*When* are we going to move?" Brother wanted to know.

"Tomorrow, bright and early," Mama told him. "The moving bears will be here first thing in the morning."

That night, as Brother bedded
down in his corner of the cave,
he wondered what it would be like
to leave his old neighborhood
and his old friends.

He wondered what it would be like
to move into a new neighborhood,
making new friends.

And then he began to wonder if
he would ever fall asleep. And
just when it began to seem that
he never would, he did.

The next morning, the moving bears came with their big truck and began moving the Bear family's things out of the cave.

"Everything goes!" said Papa.

And everything did.
The moving bears
were very fast, but very
careful. Before long,
the cave was empty.

Then, after a fond farewell look at their old home, the Bear family said good-bye to their friends and neighbors, got into their car, and headed down the mountain. The big moving truck followed.

Down, down the mountainside they went.
After a few tight spots and a few wrong
turns, they were in the rich green forest
of the valley.

"Look at that forest!" said Papa.
"Now I shall have plenty
of wood to cut."

They passed farms
with fine fields.

"And look at that
rich brown soil!
What a vegetable
garden I'll have!"
said Mama.

Brother was on the lookout for friends and playmates. But all he saw were a frog and some butterflies. And they didn't look very friendly.

"Get ready!" said Papa, as they turned onto a sunny dirt road. "Just around this bend is our new home!"

"But, it's a tree!" said Brother.

"A tree *house!*" said Papa. "A fine tree house—with a downstairs, and an upstairs, and an attic . . . and even a room of your own!"

It was, indeed, a fine house—a whole house hollowed out of a great oak.

It did need work—the paint was old, there were some broken steps, and some of the bark was loose—but Mama and Papa had great plans for fixing it up.

As the movers took the Bears'
things into their new home, the
Bears imagined what it would
look like when it was all fixed.
It was going to be very
beautiful.

They were so busy imagining, that they didn't notice they had company. Their new neighbors had come with gifts of welcome. There were rabbits with carrot stew, bird and squirrel families with seeds and nuts, and a number of bear families with honeycombs, wild berries—and lots of cubs to make friends with.

The Bear family felt very welcome in their new neighborhood. That night they went to bed very tired, but very happy.

And when they got their tree house all
fixed up, it was just about perfect!